How to be a hero

This book is not like others you have read. This is a choose-your-own-destiny book where YOU are the hero of this adventure.

Each section of this book is numbered. At the end of most sections, you will have to make a choice. Each choice will take you to a different section of the book.

If you choose correctly, you will succeed. But be careful. If you make a bad choice, you may have to start the adventure again. If this happens, make sure you learn from your mistake!

Go to the next page to start your adventure. And remember, don't be a zero, be a hero!

It is the Age of the Warlords in Japan, 500 years ago. You are a samurai in the service of Lord Oda. Samurai normally come from noble families, and your parents are poor farmers. But through your fighting skills, you have risen through the ranks of his army to become the leader of Oda's samurai. He has recently adopted you as his son.

Lord Oda supports the Shōgun, the emperor's war chief, who is trying to end the long wars between rival warlords and their clans. He has left you in charge of his castle, Azuchi, while he attends a temple ceremony in the capital city, Kyoto.

Here, he will pay his respects by bowing to the Shōgun to show his loyalty.

Go to 1.

1

You return from hunting to find that your adopted younger sister Ama, who was travelling with Lord Oda, has returned with terrible news.

"Our father and his bodyguard never reached Kyoto," she says. "They were ambushed by assassins paid for by the warlord Mitsu. I, alone, escaped."

You are stunned. You look around at your fellow samurai. Many are weeping.

"Lord Mitsu is our master now," says your deputy Nori. "We should ask him to let us into his service."

To agree with Nori, go to 13.
To disagree, go to 26.

2

"You will help us!" you tell Hanzo angrily, "whether you like it or not!"

In reply, Hanzo flings the stew in your face. The hot spices sting your eyes. By the time you can see again, the ninja has escaped.

"Forget him," you tell Ama and Niro, angrily wiping stew from your face. "He's more trouble than he's worth."

Go to 14.

3

After several hours, Hanzo returns.

"I have news," he says. "Mitsu has agreed to make peace with the Shōgun. He has invited him to sign a treaty and watch a Noh play."

Nori is confused. "A no-play? If it's not a play, what is it?"

"Not a 'no' play," Ama explains, "a 'Noh' play. It's traditional. The actors wear masks."

"Mitsu cannot be trusted," you say. "He killed Lord Oda and I'm sure he plans to kill the Shōgun."

"I agree," says Hanzo. "But this gives us a way into the castle. You capture the actors and take their places. Then you can get into the castle wearing their masks without being recognised."

To disagree with Hanzo's plan, go to 15.
To agree to it, go to 29.

4

At your orders, your followers shed their disguises and charge towards the castle, yelling battle cries.

But the castle walls are strong and high, and its guards are alert. You are met with a hail of arrows. Heavily armed samurai pour from the castle gate. You are about to be overwhelmed.

Go to 47.

5

"Ninjas are experts in stealth attack," you say. "A ninja can get us into the castle undetected. But where can we find one?"

"I know one who lives here," says Nori. "But he is a rascal and a thief."

To meet this ninja, go to 41.
To try to find a more trustworthy ally, go to 14.

6

"We must keep our swords," you tell Hanzo. "And we will hide them under our robes."

"Then you're on your own."

And as quick as the wind, Hanzo vanishes.

You have no choice but to continue on. The castle guards bow as you approach. As custom demands, you bow in return. Nori's hidden sword clatters to the floor.

"Seize them!" Your friends are taken prisoner. You have no armour, and dozens of armed swordsmen press forward to attack you.

Go to 47.

7

You raise your sword and charge towards Mitsu. His assassins close in to defend him.

But the Shōgun thinks *you* are attacking him, and calls for his guards. They rush to his defence. Now you are facing two bands of enemies instead of one! There are far too many of them for you to fight.

Go to 47.

8

You pass the great red torii gate into the shrine. The priest greets you and takes you to the inner hall where a beautiful katana sword rests on an altar.

"This sword is called Kusa," says the priest. "It is one of the greatest treasures of Japan. Your master, Lord Oda, left it here for safekeeping. Now I offer it to you, to avenge him."

You reach for the sword, but stop as the priest begins to speak again.

"It is a mighty sword, but it has another

power. If your life is in danger, grasp the hilt and call on Futen, God of the Wind. You will find yourself back in this time and place."

You thank the priest, take the sword and return to your fellow samurai.

Go to 19.

9

"We are bandits," you tell the guard commander. "We heard there was treasure in this castle, but we did not expect it to be so well-guarded. Spare us, and we will serve your master."

"Lord Mitsu has no need of carrion such as you," sneers the guard commander. He raises his sword and orders his men, "Attack!"

To fight Mitsu's men, go to 40.
To surrender, go to 27.

10

You threaten Hanzo with your sword.

"You're in no position to make demands."

Hanzo grins, and throws something that looks like an egg. It smashes on the floor.

There is a sudden flash, and the room fills with smoke that tears at your throat. When it clears, and you have wiped your streaming eyes, Hanzo is nowhere to be seen.

Go to 14.

11

"We must warn the Shōgun!" you cry.

You and your followers burst from cover and run towards the Shōgun, shouting and waving your arms.

But the Shōgun's bodyguard are nervous. With a cry of "Bandits!" they let loose a swarm of arrows at you. You have only a second to save yourself.

Go to 47.

12

You draw your sword and, stepping around the curtain, attack the assassins. They draw hidden weapons and fight you off.

Mitsu cries, "Stop him! He will kill the Shōgun!"

There is no time to tell the Shōgun the truth. The assassins close in on you. There is only one escape.

Go to 47.

13

You bow your head. "What else can we do?"

Ama is furious. "Mitsu is a traitor! If you go to serve him, who will avenge our father?"

You realise Ama is right.

Go to 26.

14

"We will get nowhere with the aid of such a ruffian," you say. "I will find someone more trustworthy to help us."

You set out alone to find a more respectable ninja, but the townspeople look on you with suspicion. Someone reports you to the castle and you are arrested as a vagrant.

You are taken to the castle, where the guard commander, his arm in a bloodstained sling, recognises you. "I know this man! He is one of Lord Oda's samurai. Deal with him!"

The nearest guard has your sword, Kusa. You snatch it from him.

Go to 47.

15

"I want no part of this foolery!" roars Nori.

"We're not actors," you tell Hanzo. "Your plan is ridiculous."

Hanzo gives you a stubborn glare. "You'll never take the castle by storm. Disguise is the ninja way. Swallow your precious samurai dignity and do as I say."

"It is an opportunity sent from the gods," says Ama. "We must try it."

You sigh. "Very well."

Go to 29.

16

"We will never take the castle by daylight," you say. "We need darkness and secrecy to confuse our enemies."

You find a hideout in an abandoned building. As darkness falls, you prepare to attack the castle.

To attack wearing samurai armour, go to 36.

If you would rather make a stealthy approach, go to 45.

17

You give Ama a nod.

"Hanzo," she said, "my father was your friend. He gave you work. He lent you money for your family."

Hanzo scowls. "Aww, you had to bring that up." He shakes his head sadly. "All right. I still think you're mad, but I'll help you for Lord Oda's sake." He grins. "And a very big fee!"

When you have agreed a fee, Hanzo says, "I'll go and spy out the castle to find a way in."

You wonder whether you can trust your new ninja ally.

To decide you can, go to 46.
To decide you can't, go to 38.

18

"Samurai!" you call, "help me find the traitor—"

You break off. Your cries have drawn Mitsu to you. He suddenly appears out of the darkness, catching you unawares and smashing the sword out of your hand. Disarmed and helpless, you have only one means of escape as Mitsu raises his sword to strike.

Go to 47.

19

Ama and your men are waiting, impatient to begin their quest. Mitsu will be at his castle, Sakamoto, but how can you reach him without being stopped by his men?

To go to Sakamoto in disguise, go to 43.
To go as samurai warriors, go to 30.

20

"Now!" you cry. "Attack!"

With their commander down, the guards pause, but only for a moment. As they fight back, reinforcements arrive. You are outnumbered!

Go to 47.

21

"We can't spare men to guard prisoners," you say. "Let them go."

But as soon as the actors are released they run back to the road. Catching up with the marching soldiers, they complain that they have been attacked by bandits who have stolen their costumes.

The soldiers run into the woods to attack you and your men. One throws a spear, which you have no time to dodge. There is only one way to avoid your fate.

Go to 47.

22

"We are the samurai of Lord Oda!" you cry. "We seek vengeance!"

The guard commander points his sword at you and your followers. "Seize them!"

You fight bravely, but the odds against you are too great. There is only one escape.

Go to 47.

23

"We must be on stage, and ready to take action together," you tell Ama. You check the opening lines of the play and turn to your men. "I will begin the play. When I say the word 'mountains', you deal with Mitsu's assassins — but leave the traitor to me!"

Ama looks unhappy, but does not argue. Your men put on their masks and take their places.

You step onto the stage. "The wind is gusting across Miho Bay," you say. "Clouds rise over the beautiful distant mountains..."

At the word 'mountains', your men draw their weapons.

The Shōgun stands. "What is the meaning of this? Put up your swords!" he orders.

To ignore the Shōgun and attack Mitsu, go to 7.

To explain to the Shōgun, go to 44.

24

"To seek help from a spy and a thief would dishonour us," you reply.

Ama is furious. "Is your honour more precious to you than avenging our father?"

You realise that Ama is right. "No," you agree. "And besides, we are already dishonoured. We will deal with a ninja, if it helps us reach our goal."

Go to 5.

25

"Ama!" you cry, bending down to help her.

Ama pushes your hand away. "Never mind me!" she cries. "Look out!"

You realise that you have made a terrible mistake in taking your eyes off your opponent.

Mitsu laughs. "Sentimental fool!"

You look up to see that he is bringing his sword down on you. You are helpless.

Go to 47.

26

"I would never have believed that Lord Oda's men could be so faint-hearted," you say. "The samurai code says that murder must not go unpunished."

"But our lord is dead," protests Nori. "Without a lord, we will no longer be samurai. We will be masterless rōnin — little better than bandits."

You shrug. "Then that is what we will be. Mitsu and his samurai are based at Sakamoto castle. We will go there. We will find Mitsu and bring him to justice. Lord Oda must be avenged!"

Your fellow samurai roar their approval of your plan.

Ama raises her head proudly. "And I will go with you!"

To protect your younger sister and refuse to take her, go to 39.

To agree to take Ama along, go to 32.

27

"We surrender!" you cry.

"Lord Mitsu takes no prisoners," scoffs the guard commander. His men fall on you like locusts. There is only one escape.

Go to 47.

28

Hanzo orders hot, spicy stew. When it arrives, you explain to him that you need his help to get into Lord Mitsu's castle.

Hanzo puts down his chopsticks and stares at you. "You're mad!" he scoffs. "How do you think you're going to get in there?"

"That's what we need you to tell us," you say. "You're supposed to be a ninja — or is eating the only thing you're good at?"

Hanzo glares. "It can't be done! I won't help you."

Ama sees that you are getting angry.

"Let me try to persuade him," she says.

To force Hanzo to help you, go to 2.
To let Ama speak to him, go to 17.

29

You and your men set out to find the actors.

You lay an ambush where the road to Sakamoto passes through a deep, wooded valley. No sooner are you in position than you hear approaching hoofbeats.

But when the travellers come into view, you see that they are not the Noh actors, but the Shōgun and his escort. They are riding towards Mitsu's castle.

To stick to your plan, go to 42.

To warn the Shōgun of Mitsu's treachery, go to 11.

30

"A samurai does not creep about in disguise," you say. "Arm yourselves!"

You set out along the road to Sakamoto. But you have not gone far before one of Mitsu's war bands spots you and charges to the attack.

You fight bravely, but you are few in number. There is only one way out!

Go to 47.

You know that if you try to help Ama, Mitsu will cut you down. You try to rush him, but Mitsu reaches into a pouch at his waist and pulls out a handful of rice. He scatters it on the planks of the bridge. You slip on the grains and fall heavily, losing your sword.

Mitsu laughs. "Goodbye, samurai!"

As he prepares to strike, Ama snatches her dagger from her belt. She stabs Mitsu in the foot. As he yells in agony, you surge to your feet and shoulder-charge him off the bridge and into the lake.

Mitsu sits in the shallow water, splashing like a stranded fish. His heavy armour makes it impossible for him to rise.

"Get me out of here!" he roars.

"You can stay where you are," you tell him, "until the Shōgun's men arrive. They can fish you out, and bring you to justice!"

Go to 50.

32

"Very well," you say. "Join us, if you wish."

Nori and his fellow guards grumble at your decision. This is no mission for the daughter of Lord Oda. But younger samurai, who have trained with Ama, agree with your decision.

"We go to avenge her father," says one. "She has the right to join us."

One of the palace servants appears and falls to his knees. "A Shinto priest has sent a message. He wants you to visit him at his shrine."

To agree to visit the priest, go to 8.
To refuse, go to 48.

33

"You're right. We can't trust Hanzo," you tell Nori. "We will try your plan."

Leaving your samurai armour at the hideout, you lead your men up to the castle gate and ask to see the commander of the guard.

The commander arrives with his arm in a bloodstained sling. He recognises you instantly.

"You are no mercenaries — you are Lord Oda's men!" He orders his guards to attack.

You are heavily outnumbered by armoured guards. There is no hope of victory, or escape.

Go to 47.

You raise your voice. "Retreat!"

You and the others head back to the hideout. The pursuing guards soon give up the chase.

"Attacking the castle will not work," you say, "especially now the guards are expecting it. We need a new strategy."

Ama speaks up. "We need help from a ninja."

To agree with Ama, go to 5.
To refuse to take such a dishonourable step, go to 24.

You lock up the players in a disused watermill. You leave one of your men to guard them. Then you take the ox-cart, put on the costumes and masks of the Noh actors, and head for the castle.

Hanzo joins you as you enter the town.

"Good. Now, you must hide your long swords in the cart: otherwise, they'll give you away."

Your men are shocked. The katana sword is the *soul of the warrior*. A samurai should never let it leave his side.

To ignore Hanzo's advice, go to 6.
To accept it, go to 49.

36

Your heavy armour slows you down. Lanterns and watchfires glitter on its polished surfaces. As you run, it clatters loudly in the still night air.

You stop your men. "This is no good. The guards will know we're coming. Take off your armour — surprise will serve us better than strength."

Go to 45.

37

As you stalk Mitsu through the garden, you hear footsteps. Running silently towards them, you come across Mitsu. He is standing on a wooden bridge that crosses a lake.

He glares at you. "You have no master. You have no honour. You are no samurai."

"At least," you reply, "I am no traitor."

With a snarl, Mitsu draws his sword and you fight.

Ama appears on the other side of the bridge and charges into the fray. Mitsu delivers her a vicious backhanded blow with his sword hilt and she falls.

To help Ama, go to 25.
To continue your attack on Mitsu, go to 31.

38

"I don't trust you," you tell Hanzo. "You'll stay here, under guard, until we need you."

"I don't think so!" Hanzo kicks over the table that stands between you. Fast and as slippery as an eel, he makes for the door.

With Ama and Nori, you chase him outside and run into a squad of guards. Hanzo points at you. "These people are traitors!"

The guards rush at you, weapons raised.

Go to 47.

39

"This is a task for men," you tell Ama.

She glares at you. "This is a task for samurai — and I have trained as a warrior, just as you have." With that, she draws her sword and attacks you. You are taken by surprise and fall back, barely able to parry her attacks.

You hold up a hand in a gesture of peace.

Go to 32.

40

You and your men fight desperately against a superior force of guards.

As you and Nori fight back-to-back, you ask him, "Have you seen Ama?"

"No!" he says. "You were a fool to bring that girl along!"

At that moment, the guard commander cries out in pain and falls, an arrow jutting from his shoulder. You look around to see Ama, her bow still raised. She made the shot that has given you some breathing space.

"What was that about not trusting my sister?" you ask Nori.

Nori bows to you and Ama, repentant and contrite.

To fight on, go to 20.
To try to make your escape, go to 34.

41

Nori leads you and Ama to a poor eating-house, where you meet the ninja, Hanzo. He is a villainous-looking rogue, dirty and ill-dressed. You tell him you need his help.

He gives you a cheeky grin. "I will think about it — if you buy me some food."

You are angered by Hanzo's lack of respect.

To do as Hanzo asks, go to 28.
To refuse, go to 10.

42

"Let them go by," you order. "The Shōgun's men will not listen to disgraced rōnin."

Shortly afterwards, you hear more hoofbeats, and the Noh actors appear. Some are walking, and others riding on an ox-cart.

Your attack takes them completely by surprise. Soon, they are your prisoners.

You hear the sound of marching feet. "The Shōgun's soldiers," you say, "following behind the riders!"

At your orders, the actors are driven into the woods.

"What shall we do with them?" asks Nori.

To order your men to let the players go, go to 21.

To lock them up under guard, go to 35.

"We are no longer samurai," you say. "We have no master now. We are rōnin. We will travel as merchants to avoid suspicion, but we will carry our armour with us and be prepared to fight."

You make your preparations, and set off in your disguise. Several days later you find yourself in the town of Sakamoto. The castle rises above the town: it is large with strong walls and heavily guarded.

To storm the castle in a surprise attack, go to 4.

To wait for nightfall, go to 16.

44

You tear off your mask and bow to the Shōgun.

"My lord, Mitsu is a traitor. He killed Lord Oda, and plans to kill you too!"

Mitsu's assassins draw their weapons, but the Shōgun's guards, warned of their plans, come to your aid. Mitsu's thugs are quickly overpowered. However, in the confusion, Mitsu escapes through a nearby doorway. You give chase and find yourself in a garden.

To call your men to help you search for Mitsu, go to 18.

To stalk the traitor yourself, go to 37.

45

Without the weight of your armour, you reach the castle quickly and succeed in climbing the walls. But once you are inside the castle, guards appear from every doorway. You have walked into a trap!

The captain of the guard approaches, sword raised. "Who are you?"

To tell the truth, go to 22.

To hide your true identity, go to 9.

46

You nod. "Very well."

Hanzo disappears. He is gone for so long that you start to think he has broken his agreement and means to betray you.

"He's not coming back," says Nori angrily. "Forget him. We should bluff our way into the castle pretending to be mercenary soldiers, seeking employment from Mitsu."

"No," says Ama. "We should trust Hanzo."

To agree with Ama, go to 3.
To agree with Nori, go to 33.

47

You hold the sword Kusa's hilt in both hands. "Lord Futen, come to my aid!"

There is a mighty rush of wind that buffets your ears. You fall to your knees and find yourself back in the shrine of the Shinto priest.

"It seems you have met with misfortune," he says calmly. "Begin your journey again but choose more mindfully in future."

Go to 19.

48

"We have no need of priests," you say.

But your men are angry. "You will bring us bad luck," says one.

"You have no respect for the gods," says another. "You have no honour. We will not follow you."

You realise these men speak for all.

"I only wished to save time," you say. "I apologise: I will go and see the priest."

Go to 8.

49

"Our katanas are too big to hide," you say. "Leave them in the cart."

At the castle, one of the guards gives Nori a suspicious look. "You look pretty strong," he says, "for an actor."

"He works out," says Hanzo quickly.

Fooled by your disguise, the guard waves you through.

Hanzo grins. "I got you in — as promised. Good luck, samurai." He vanishes.

You retrieve your swords from the cart and get ready to go on stage. "I feel like a fool in these robes," Nori grumbles.

You ignore him and peer out through the curtains at the audience. The Shōgun is sitting in the front row alongside Mitsu. The men sitting around them look suspiciously big and burly.

Ama catches her breath. "Those are the men Mitsu sent to kill my father. They are hired assassins — they will kill the Shōgun!"

To make plans to deal with the assassins, go to 23.

To attack the assassins at once, go to 12.

50

You return to the theatre, and find the Shōgun. You tell him of Mitsu's treachery.

The Shōgun sends his guards to arrest Mitsu. "It seems," he says, "that though I have lost my friend Lord Oda, I have gained new allies in his children." He turns to Ama. "I appoint you to my personal guard." Ama bows, unable to hide a beam of delight.

The Shōgun indicates your men. "You are no longer masterless rōnin; you are samurai, in my service." He claps you on the shoulder. "And you, my friend, are promoted to the rank of general in my army. You are a true hero!"

I HERO Quiz

Test yourself with this special quiz. It has been designed to see how much you remember about the book you've just read. Can you get all five answers right?

Question 1

Who brings you the terrible news about your adpoted father, Lord Oda?

A   Mitsu

B   Ama

C   your father's bodyguard

D   the Shōgun

Question 2

What is the name of the priest's katana sword?

A   Kusa

B   Futen

C   Oda

D   Hanzo

Question 3

In which town is the castle?

A   Kyoto

B   Azuchi

C   Miho Bay

D   Sakamoto

Question 4

What is your mission?

A   to join Mitsu's service

B   to bring Mistu to justice

C   to become a masterless rōnin

D   to seek advice from the priest

Question 5

How does the Shōgun reward your loyalty?

A   he appoints you to his personal guard

B   he gives you his sacred sword

C   he promotes you to the rank of
     general

D   he makes you a warlord

Answers:
1. B; 2. A; 3. D; 4. B and 5. C.

About the 2Steves

"The 2Steves" are one of Britain's most popular writing double acts for young people, specialising in comedy and adventure. They  perform regularly in schools and libraries, and at festivals, taking the power of words and story to audiences of all ages.

Together they have written many books, including the *Monster Hunter* series. Find out what they've been up to at: **www.the2steves.net**

About the illustrator: Judit Tondora

Judit Tondora was born in Miskolc, Hungary and now works from her countryside studio. Judit's artwork has appeared in books, comics, posters and on commercial design projects.

To find out more about her work, visit: **www.astound.us/publishing/artists/ judit-tondora**

Have you completed these I HERO adventures?

Battle with monsters in Monster Hunter:

978 1 4451 5878 5 pb
978 1 4451 5876 1 ebook

978 1 4451 5935 5 pb
978 1 4451 5933 1 ebook

978 1 4451 5936 2 pb
978 1 4451 5937 9 ebook

978 1 4451 5939 3 pb
978 1 4451 5940 9 ebook

978 1 4451 5942 3 pb
978 1 4451 5943 0 ebook

978 1 4451 5945 4 pb
978 1 4451 5946 1 ebook

Defeat all the baddies in Toons:

978 1 4451 5930 0 pb
978 1 4451 5931 7 ebook

978 1 4451 5921 8 pb
978 1 4451 5922 5 ebook

978 1 4451 5924 9 pb
978 1 4451 5925 6 ebook

978 1 4451 5918 8 pb
978 1 4451 5919 5 ebook

Also by the 2Steves...

978 1 4451 5985 0

Tip can't believe his luck when he mysteriously wins tickets to see his favourite team in the cup final. But there's a surprise in store ...

978 1 4451 5892 1

Big baddie Mr Butt Hedd is in hot pursuit of the space cadets and has tracked them down for Lord Evil. But can Jet, Tip and Boo Hoo find a way to escape in a cunning disguise?

978 1 4451 5988 1

Jet and Tip get a new command from Master Control to intercept some precious cargo. It's time to become space pirates!

978 1 4451 5979 9

The goodies intercept a distress signal and race to the rescue. Then some 8-legged fiends appear ... Tip and Jet realise it's a trap!